The Need for Speed

Frank was the last to try the obstacle course. He took the slalom so slowly that his bike wobbled. But he reached the end without hitting any cones.

"Good going, Frank," Mike Mendez called.

Biff Hooper laughed. "Even babies can ride slow," he said. "Winners ride fast. How about it, Hardy? Want to race? Or are you too scared?"

"Sure, Biff, I'll race you," Frank replied. "Down to the creek and back?"

"You got it, dude," Biff said.

The two boys lined up. The other kids chanted, "On your mark . . . Get set . . . GO!"

The Hardy Boys® are: The Clues Brothers™

Available from MINSTREL Books

The Hardy Boys® are:

The Clues Brothers™

The Bike Race Ruckus

#17

Franklin W. Dixon

Illustrated by
Marcy Ramsey

A
MINSTREL®
BOOK

Published by POCKET BOOKS
New York   London   Toronto   Sydney   Singapore

This book is a work of fiction. Names, characters, places and incidents are products of the author's imagination or are used fictitiously. Any resemblance to actual events or locales or persons living or dead is entirely coincidental.

A MINSTREL PAPERBACK Original

 A Minstrel Book published by
POCKET BOOKS, a division of Simon & Schuster Inc.
1230 Avenue of the Americas, New York, NY 10020

Copyright © 2000 by Simon & Schuster Inc.

ISBN: 0-671-04041-3

First Minstrel Books printing April 2000

10 9 8 7 6 5 4 3 2 1

THE HARDY BOYS ARE: THE CLUES BROTHERS is a trademark of Simon & Schuster Inc.

THE HARDY BOYS, A MINSTREL BOOK and colophon are registered trademarks of Simon & Schuster Inc.

Cover art by Frank Sofo

Printed in the U.S.A.

PHX/

1

Deals on Wheels

Hey, Frank! Watch this!" Eight-year-old Joe Hardy pedaled quickly across the baseball diamond. He turned left and threw his weight to the side. His bike swerved and slid to a stop. The tires kicked up a thick cloud of dust.

"Yuck!" Frank Hardy, Joe's nine-year-old brother, shielded his face with his hands. The dust turned his jeans and T-shirt yellow-brown. He started to brush the dust off. "You'd better not try that on Saturday, Joe," he warned. "The judges might throw you out for choking them."

"Aw," Joe said. "I thought it was a pretty cool trick."

It was Thursday afternoon. Frank and Joe had come to the park after school. They wanted to practice for the Bike Jamboree on Saturday. Lots of kids in Bayport were planning to compete. The grand prize was a super twenty-speed mountain bike.

Frank saw Chet Morton ride into the park. He waved. Chet was in Frank's fourth-grade class at Bayport Elementary School. He was good friends with both Frank and Joe.

"Whew," Chet panted as he rode up. "This training is hard work. I need a boost."

He reached in his backpack and pulled out a candy bar wrapped in shiny foil. He opened the foil and took a bite.

"Candy?" Joe asked. "You call that training?"

"It's not candy, it's an energy bar," Chet

told him. "All the top athletes use them."

Frank looked at the wrapper. "It's mostly chocolate and sugar," he reported.

Chet took another bite. "Right. Fast energy. Everybody knows that. I feel stronger already."

"Just in time," Joe said. "Here comes a whole bunch of kids. Look—Tony has a stack of traffic cones. We can set up a slalom."

Half a dozen kids rode up and stopped. Frank knew most of them from school. Tony Prito and Mike Mendez were in the same third-grade class as Joe. Tanya Wilkins was in fourth grade, but not in Frank's class. They were friends from karate school.

A girl with a snub nose and freckles smiled at Frank and said, "Hi."

Frank remembered seeing her in the hall the last few weeks, but he didn't know her. Her brown hair was pulled back in a ponytail. On her T-shirt was a cartoon bear and the words *Jellystone Park*. Her bike looked too big for her.

"Hi," he replied. "I'm Frank. That's my brother, Joe. You're new at school, aren't you?"

The girl nodded. "Uh-huh. We just moved here from Arizona. My name is Debbie."

"Debbie's in Mr. Levy's class with me," Tanya added.

Frank started to ask Debbie how she liked Bayport. But Tony said, "Hey, guys, let's get to work. Frank, Joe? How about helping me lay out a slalom course?"

"Did you say a salami course?" Chet joked. "I'll have a double serving."

Frank and Joe groaned. Chet was famous for always being hungry.

"Here, I'll help you," Debbie offered. "I need to practice. I really want to win that bike."

"Sure. Me, too," Joe said with a grin. "But I bet the jamboree will be fun even if we don't win."

Frank took the stack of orange rubber cones from Tony. He passed some to Joe and some to Debbie.

"We'll set them in a straight line," Frank explained. "Then we ride our bikes in and out like a snake. The closer you come to the cones, the more points you get. But if you knock any over, you lose points."

"Oh, right," Debbie said. "I do that on skates." She took her cones and walked across the field, placing them about five feet apart. Frank and Joe set theirs in line with hers. As soon as they were done, Tony got back on his bike.

"Here comes Tony the Rocket!" he yelled.

Tony started pedaling way back to get up speed. He passed the first cone on the left. Then he swerved right to clear the second cone. When he tried to turn back, he had already gone too far. His front wheel hit the third cone. The rubber cone went bouncing across the field.

"Oops!" Tony said. "This isn't as easy as I thought." He got off his bike and put the cone back in place.

"My turn," Tanya announced. She straddled her bike and started to push off.

5

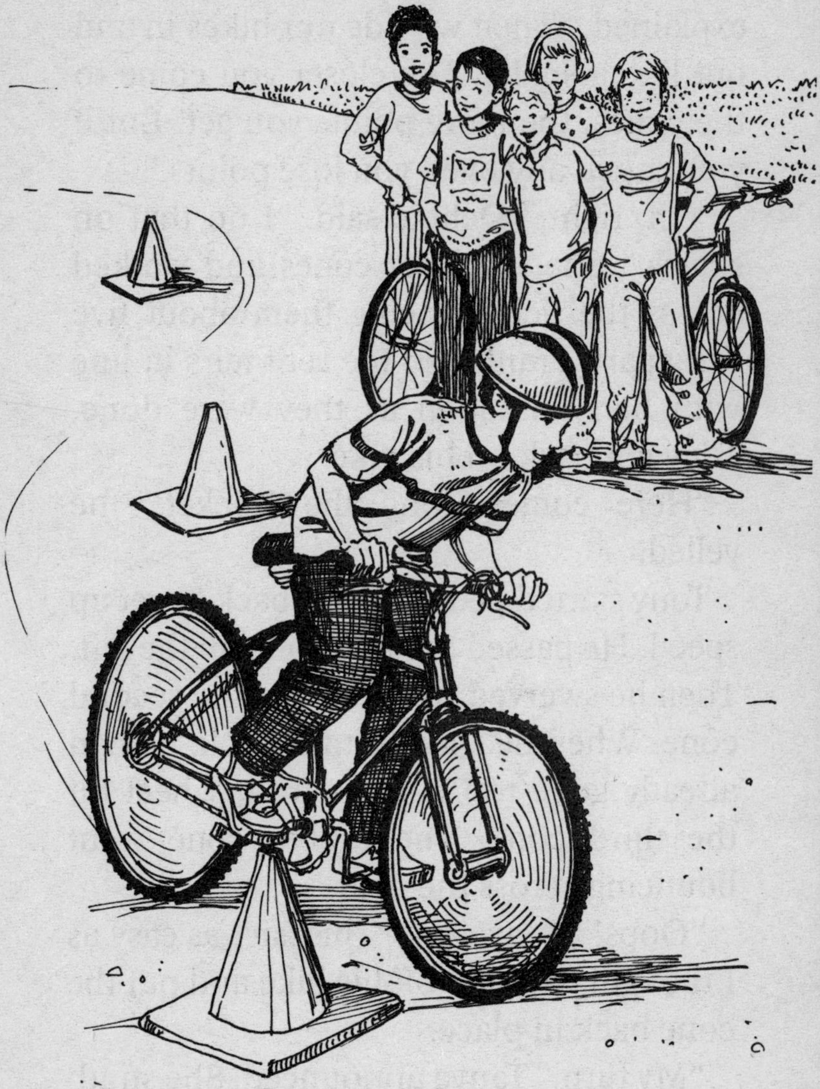

"Yee-ha!" someone shouted from across the field.

Frank turned to look.

A guy on a bike came racing along the slalom line. He didn't even try to dodge in and out. Instead, as he passed each cone, he kicked it over. He braked to a stop right in front of the group of watching kids.

"I win," he announced. "I got every one of them!"

"Zack," Joe said loudly to Frank. "I should have guessed."

Zack Jackson was the biggest bully at Bayport Elementary School. He and his friends called themselves the Zack Pack.

Zack glared at Joe. "You got a problem, Hardy-har-har?" he demanded.

One time at the movies Joe had dumped his bag of popcorn over Zack's head. Zack still had it in for Joe because of that.

"No, Zack," Frank said. *"You've* got a problem. You just knocked over our slalom course. Now you have to set it up again."

"Oh, yeah? Who's going to make me?" Zack demanded.

Frank and Joe moved closer to him. So did the other kids. Zack looked at the circle of unfriendly faces. "Okay, okay," he said. "Can't you guys take a joke?"

While Zack was replacing the cones, Biff Hooper and Brett Marks showed up. They were part of the Zack Pack, too.

"Hey, dweebs," Brett called. "You practicing for the jamboree? Don't bother. Come Saturday, it's going to be me first and all of you nowhere!"

"Too bad it's not a hot-air contest," Chet replied. "You'd win for sure."

Brett clenched his fists. "Watch it, Morton," he growled.

"Ooh, help, somebody!" Chet held out his hand and made it shake. "I'm trembling all over."

The other kids laughed. Brett scowled at them and stomped away.

"Oh, look," Tanya said. "Keiko has her new puppy with her. It is *so* cute!"

Everybody ran over to see. Frank petted the pup. "What's its name?" he asked.

"I called her Cinnamon," Keiko told him. "Because of her color."

They played with Cinnamon for a few minutes. Then Tony said, "If we want to practice slalom, we'd better do it now. I have to take the cones when I go home."

"Me first," Brett announced. He pushed past Debbie and dashed back to his bike. He started to climb on. Then he gave an angry shout. "Okay, who's the joker? I'll get you for this!"

Brett was pointing at the front wheel of his bike. Frank looked. One of the brake pads was covered with gooey pink bubble gum.

2

Gumming Up the Works

Morton, you wuss!" Brett yelled. "You wrecked my brakes. I'll get you for this!"

Brett reached out to grab Chet. Chet backed away.

"I didn't do anything," Chet insisted. "What's the matter with you?"

Joe and Frank stepped between Brett and Chet. "Take it easy," Joe said. "What makes you think Chet put that gum on your brakes?"

Brett scowled at Joe. "You saw him arguing with me before," he said. "Who else has it in for me?"

"Who doesn't?" Tony muttered. Brett and the others in the Zack Pack had done mean things to a lot of kids.

"*Somebody* put the gum there," Zack said. "If it wasn't Morton, who was it?"

"This sounds like a case for the Clues Brothers," Tanya said.

The Clues Brothers was a name their friends had given Joe and Frank. Their dad, Fenton Hardy, was a private detective. They were learning to solve mysteries, too.

"Brett?" Joe asked. "Did you see any gum on your brake before we all went to look at Keiko's puppy?"

"What kind of dumb question is that?" Brett retorted. "You think I ride around with bubble gum on my brakes?"

"But you did see it as soon as you got on your bike, right?" Frank asked.

"Right. So what?" Brett grunted.

Joe turned to Chet. "You were one of the first to go over to see the puppy, weren't you? And one of the last to come back?"

"Hey, that's right!" Chet exclaimed.

"That means I couldn't have put the gum there!"

"So the Clues Brothers' buddy has an alibi," Zack sneered. "Very convenient."

Joe ignored him. "Look," he said. He bent down and picked up a little square of paper. "It's a gum wrapper. Bigger Bubbles bubble gum. Anybody heard of it?"

"I have," Chet said. "I tried it once. It's supposed to taste like strawberries. Pretty gross."

"I like the way it tastes," Debbie announced. "And it really does make bigger bubbles. But not many stores carry it. I've got a piece right here."

Debbie reached into the pocket of her backpack. Then Joe noticed her get a funny expression on her face. She said, "Oops, I forgot. I left it at home."

Frank put his face near the brakes on Brett's bike and sniffed. Then he took the wrapper from Joe and sniffed that. "Yup," he said. "They smell the same. Strawberries."

"Whenever you chew gum, the flavor goes away pretty fast," Joe pointed out. "If you can still smell that gum, it wasn't chewed for very long."

Frank nodded. "Good point, Joe. Somebody chewed it just enough to make it sticky, then stuck it on Brett's brake."

"How long would that take?" Joe wondered. "Anybody have a stick of gum?"

"I do," Chet volunteered. "I always carry a supply of snacks, just in case. It's not bubble gum, though."

"That's okay. When I say go, unwrap the gum and chew it until it's soft." Joe looked at his watch. When the second hand got close to the twelve, he said, "Ready . . . go!"

Chet ripped off the wrapper and stuck the gum in his mouth. He dropped the wrapper on the ground. He chewed half a dozen times, fast, then took the wad of gum out. He held it up between his thumb and index finger.

"You keep away from my bike!" Brett warned. Chet grinned at him.

"Only seven seconds," Joe reported. "That's amazing!"

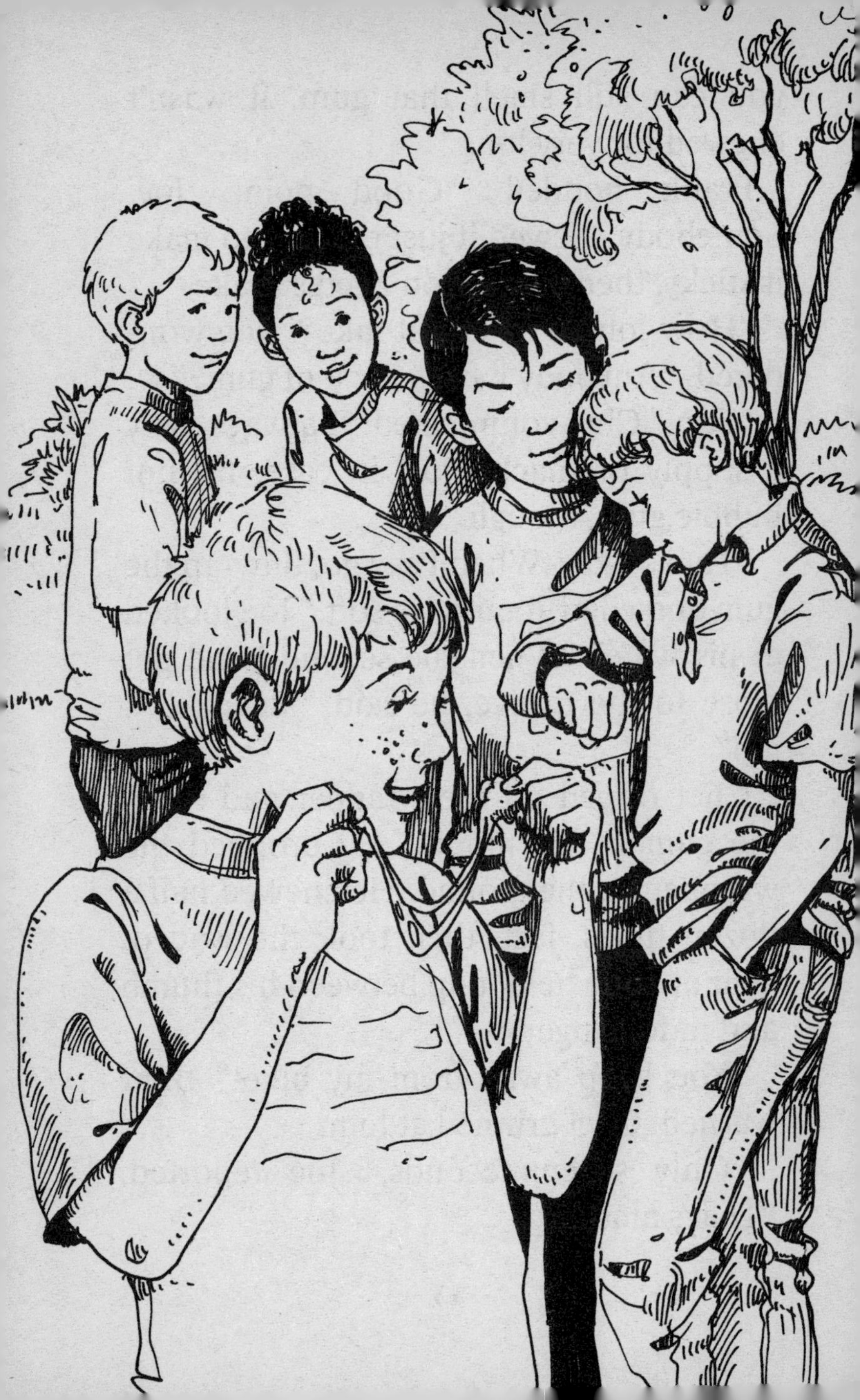

"So it didn't have to take very long," Frank said. "How about it? Did any of you see somebody fiddle with the bike? Even for a second?"

"Nope," Tanya said.

"Uh-uh," Tony said, shaking his head.

"Not me," Chet added.

"Er . . . ," Debbie said. "I bumped into that bike. It almost fell over. I had to catch it."

"That's right, I remember," Mike said. "You stopped, and I nearly ran into you."

"But I didn't know whose it was," Debbie added quickly. "And today's the first time I met— What's your name again?"

Brett scowled at her and didn't answer.

"That's Brett," Joe said.

". . . the first time I met Brett," Debbie continued. "So why would I mess up his bike?"

"Wait till you get to know him," Mike cracked. "You'll find all kinds of reasons."

"*Arrgh!*" Brett made a lunge at Mike. Mike ran away laughing.

Zack grabbed Brett's arm. "We're wasting our time," he said. "Forget the Clown Brothers. They won't help you. They just want to cover up for their friends."

"Well, they'd better keep their paws off my bike," Brett muttered. "I'm going to be on the lookout from now on. And come Saturday, they'll be eating my dust!"

Tony picked up his bike and said, "You guys argue all you want. I'm going to practice the slalom."

"I'm next after you," Debbie said.

The others lined up behind her. Brett opened a pouch fastened to the bike seat and took out a screwdriver. He started scraping the bubble gum off his brake pad. Joe motioned to Frank. They went off to the side.

"We ought to watch out," Joe whispered. "We're going to have the Zack Pack on our case now."

"We can handle them," Frank replied. "Besides, we were only trying to help."

"Sure, *I* know that. But do they believe it?" Joe wondered.

"Once we solve the mystery, they'll have to," Frank told him.

"Hey, you guys," Tony called. "You want to try the slalom or not? I've got to take the cones home."

Joe and Frank grabbed their bikes and got behind Tanya, the last in line.

It was Joe's turn. He decided to go fast. The first half went okay. Then he started bumping into one cone after another. He stopped his bike. "It's not my fault," he joked. "I'm riding great. But those silly things keep getting in my way!"

Frank was the last to try. He took the slalom so slowly that his bike wobbled. But he reached the end without hitting any cones.

"Good going, Frank," Mike called.

Biff laughed. "Even babies can ride slow," he said. "Winners ride fast. How about it, Hardy? Want to race? Or are you too scared?"

"Sure, Biff, I'll race you," Frank replied. "Down to the creek and back?"

"You got it, dude," Biff said.

The two boys lined up. The other kids chanted, "On your mark . . . Get set . . . GO!"

Frank shoved off and bent low over the handlebars. He sensed Biff right beside him. He concentrated on sending all his energy to the pedals. With each stroke he drew a little farther ahead.

The path entered the woods and changed from concrete to dirt. As it neared the creek, it sloped downhill. Frank picked up speed. But Biff picked up even more speed. He drew even again. Then he pulled ahead.

Biff looked back and grinned in triumph. As he did, his bike swerved left, in front of Frank. Frank twisted the handlebars to keep from running into Biff.

"Yow!" Frank felt his rear wheel start to skid. He tried to stop the skid by steering in the opposite direction.

Too late. His front wheel hit a tree root. The bike flipped. Frank flew headfirst over the handlebars.

3

A Lesson in Sportsmanship

In a flash Frank tucked his chin against his chest and hunched his shoulders. He had learned in karate class how to break a fall by rolling.

Too bad he hadn't learned how to crash into a thick, prickly bush without getting scratched!

"Frank! Frank!" an anxious voice cried. "Are you okay? Did you get hurt?"

Frank backed out of the bush and looked around. Chet's little sister, Iola, was standing on the path. She stared at him with big, scared eyes.

Biff rode his bike back and stopped. He looked scared, too. "Yeah, are you okay?" he demanded.

Frank gave himself a quick check. His helmet had protected his face, but he had some scratches on his arms and hands. His right shoulder twinged when he moved it. Otherwise, everything seemed all right. "I'm okay," he reported.

"Whew!" Biff said. "I didn't mean to cut you off. My bike kind of turned when I looked back."

"That's okay," Frank started to say.

Biff scowled. "Still, it wasn't really my fault. You should watch where you're going." He turned and rode away before Frank could answer.

"Couldn't he say he was sorry?" Iola wondered. "That's not nice."

"Forget it," Frank said. He noticed that Iola was carrying binoculars and a guide to birds. "Spotted any interesting birds?"

Iola's eyes lit up.

"You really are a detective," she said. "I saw some robins and a blue jay, and a couple of songbird nests. This kid I know saw a red-tailed hawk yesterday. I couldn't find him, though. And now it's too late. I have to get home."

"I'll walk you as far as the playground," Frank said. He picked up his bike. "Maybe your hawk will show up tomorrow."

At dinner Frank and Joe told their parents about the Bike Jamboree. Frank showed off his scratches and explained how he'd gotten them.

"That Biff!" Joe exclaimed. "I bet he ran you off the path on purpose."

"I don't think so," Frank replied. "But once he knew I wasn't hurt bad, he didn't seem sorry I'd crashed."

Joe narrowed his eyes. "Zack and his gang are so mean," he said. "I'm glad somebody messed with Brett's bike!"

"I can see why you're angry, Joe," Mr. Hardy said. "I would be, too."

Mrs. Hardy said, "It's so upsetting when other children don't play fair. Especially when somebody might get hurt."

"Still," Mr. Hardy continued, "a good sport plays fair even when his opponent doesn't. *Especially* when his opponent doesn't. You're not doing it for him. You're doing it for your own self-respect."

Joe stared down at his plate. "*I* wouldn't mess with somebody's bike," he said. "And we'll find out who did it, too. We'll make sure they don't do it again."

"We know that, dear," Mrs. Hardy said. She reached across and patted Joe's hand. "Now, who's for dessert? I made cherry cobbler."

That was a favorite of Joe's. "Yay!" he cheered. He jumped up. "I'll help clear."

The next morning, for practice, Frank and Joe rode their bikes to school. On the way, they met Chet and Iola. They had their bikes, too.

Frank noticed Iola had her binoculars with her. "Those'll come in handy," he joked. "There's quite a few weird birds at Bayport Elementary."

"I'm going straight to the park after

school," Iola said seriously. "I really want to see that hawk."

At school the four friends put their bikes in the rack at the side of the building. They were walking around to the front when Brett ran over to them. His face was bright red.

"I'll fix you, Morton," he said loudly. "You'll never mess with my bike again!"

A crowd started to gather.

Chet turned pale. "I don't know what you're talking about," he said.

"We settled this yesterday, Brett," Frank said. "Chet couldn't have put the bubble gum on your brakes. Remember?"

"I'm not talking about that," Brett retorted. "This turkey sneaked into my garage last night and let the air out of my tires."

"I did not!" Chet shouted. "Who says I did? Whoever it is, they're lying!"

"*I* say so," Brett said. "I saw somebody running away. It looked like you. I went to check. Both my bike tires were flat."

"This was last night?" Joe asked. "What time? How much light was there?"

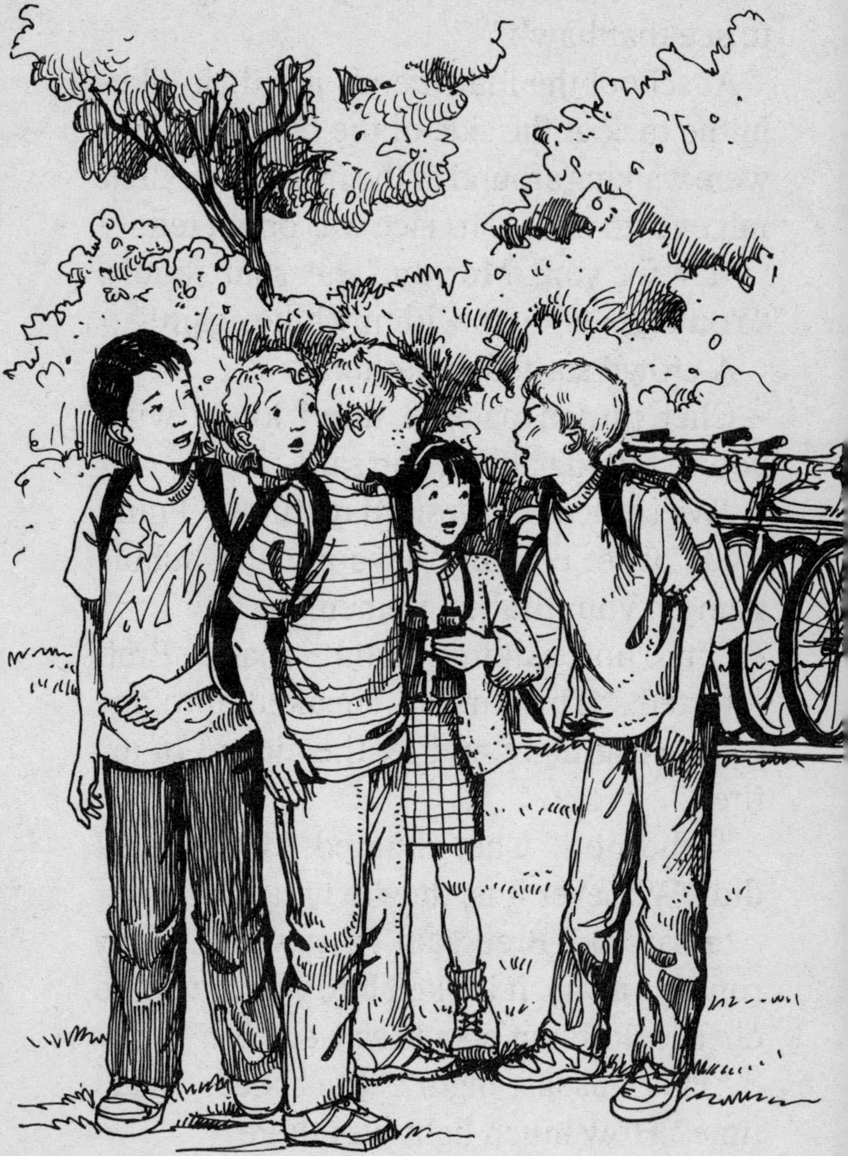

Brett hesitated. "It was about seven. It was getting dark, but there's a streetlight down the block from us."

"Seven?" Chet repeated. "That proves I'm innocent. I was eating dinner."

Iola pushed forward. "He was, too. I know. I was there. We had macaroni and cheese."

"Was the guy you saw holding a plate of macaroni and cheese?" Frank asked Brett.

The other kids laughed.

Brett's face got even redder. "It's no joke," he insisted. "Somebody's playing these tricks to keep me from winning the jamboree. And when I find out who it is, I'll flatten him!"

Brett stomped away.

Frank looked at Joe. "We'd better question all the kids who were at the park yesterday," he said. "If Brett gets any madder, he might do something really nasty."

"At the park?" Joe said. He looked puzzled. "Oh, I get it. You think it was the bubble-gum bandit who flattened his tires."

25

Frank laughed. "After all, how many enemies can one kid make, even Brett? You take the third graders, and I'll take the fourth."

Later, during recess, Frank and Joe compared notes.

"Mike and Tony were home all evening," Joe reported. "They both said we can check with their parents if we want. I think they were telling the truth. How did you do?"

"Tanya went down the block to a friend's house," Frank said. "She said she wasn't away from home long. But she *was* out. And Debbie says she was in her room all evening doing homework. She didn't see anybody or talk to anybody."

"So maybe she could have sneaked away and done it," Joe said. "And so could Tanya. But she's such a big fan of Jimmy Han and his principles of honesty. I don't think she'd pull a dirty trick on someone. Is that everybody?"

"No," Frank said with a grin. "But the

others wouldn't talk to me—Zack and Biff."

Joe stared at him. "Why would they give their buddy a flat?"

Frank shrugged. "Why would anybody? They're on our list, though. Until we cross them off, they're still suspects."

The final bell of the day rang. Frank waited for Joe in the hall near the front door.

The Zack Pack was hanging out near the bike rack. When Zack saw the Hardys coming, he said, "Watch out, guys. The Clown Brothers are on the case."

Frank and Joe ignored him. They got their bikes and walked them to the drive.

Joe climbed on. Suddenly he let out a surprised yelp. He tumbled sideways to the ground. The bike fell over on his leg.

Frank hurried to Joe and lifted the bike. The saddle post had slipped all the way down. The seat was so low now that a kindergarten kid could ride it.

4

A Low Blow from a Nut

Joe scrambled to his feet. He rubbed his elbow where he'd bumped it.

"What's the matter?" Zack called. "Did you leave your training wheels at home?"

"Yeah," Brett said. "Maybe you should trade that in on a nice trike!"

The Zack Pack laughed loudly and slapped one another on the shoulder. Other kids on their way home turned to look at Joe. Some of them laughed, too.

Joe's cheeks burned. He was sure he looked ridiculous. He took the bike from Frank.

"What happened?" Frank asked.

Joe grabbed the bike saddle. It wasn't supposed to move at all. Now it turned easily. He got down on one knee and looked under the seat.

"There's a nut that keeps the seat steady," he reported. "It was okay this morning. Now it's so loose, it's about to fall off."

"Somebody must have fiddled with it," Frank said. "Very funny, I don't think. What if you'd been riding when the seat fell down? You could have had a bad accident."

Frank stalked over to Zack and his friends. They were still laughing and making jokes about Joe and his bike.

"What do you guys know about this?" Frank demanded.

"Don't start with us, Hardy," Zack replied. "We wouldn't touch your bratty brother's bike. I bet it's got cooties."

"Yeah," Brett said. "He probably did it himself."

Frank rolled his eyes. "Let me know if

you ever decide to make sense," he retorted.

"Hey, no, that's it!" Zack exclaimed. "Joe loosened the seat so he could blame us. That way we'll stop blaming his pal for letting the air out of Brett's tires."

"That's smart, really smart," Brett said. He gave Zack a high five.

Frank turned away disgusted. Three girls from his grade were talking near the bike rack. He went over to them.

"What happened to Joe's bike?" a girl named Ellen asked.

"The seat came loose," Frank told her. "You didn't notice anybody doing anything to the bikes, did you?"

"Nope," Ellen said. "Sorry."

One of her friends said, "Hey, wait—I did. This girl was fixing a bike seat with some kind of tool. But it wasn't Joe's bike. It was her own. I know—she rode off on it."

"Who was it?" Frank asked excitedly.

"That new girl in Mr. Levy's class," she replied. "Debbie something."

"Thanks." Frank hurried back to his

bike. Joe had just finished tightening his saddle. Frank told him what he'd learned.

"Let's go find her," Joe said. "I want to know why she did it."

"We don't *know* she did it," Frank reminded him. "Remember what Dad says. A good detective always waits for proof."

Frank and Joe rode to the park. Some grown-ups were there. They were marking the trail for the cross-country race. Frank described Debbie, but the grown-ups hadn't seen her.

"I think I know where she lives," Joe announced. "I saw her last week, over on Parsons Street—a gray house with a swing set."

The shortest way to Parsons Street went down the block where Brett lived. As the Hardys rode past his house, Frank looked at the nearest streetlamp. How much light had Brett had the night before, when he saw somebody in his drive? Frank tried to peek into the garage, too, but the door was shut.

As they turned onto Parsons Street, Frank spotted Debbie. She was just getting on her bike. She saw them coming. She waited with one foot on the pedal and the other on the ground. They turned into her drive and stopped next to her.

"Hello," Debbie said in a wary voice. "What are you guys doing?"

"Not much," Frank replied. "Just riding around."

"I'm going to the park," Debbie said. "I need to practice for tomorrow. If I don't win that bike, "I don't know what!"

"Lots of kids want to win," Joe said. "I hear you had to do some work on your bike after school today."

Debbie shrugged. "No big deal. The seat was too high. I lowered it."

"That's really funny," Joe said. "You know why? Today after school, I got on my bike. The seat went all the way down. Somebody had messed with it. Somebody who had the right tool and knew how to use it."

Debbie looked from Joe to Frank and

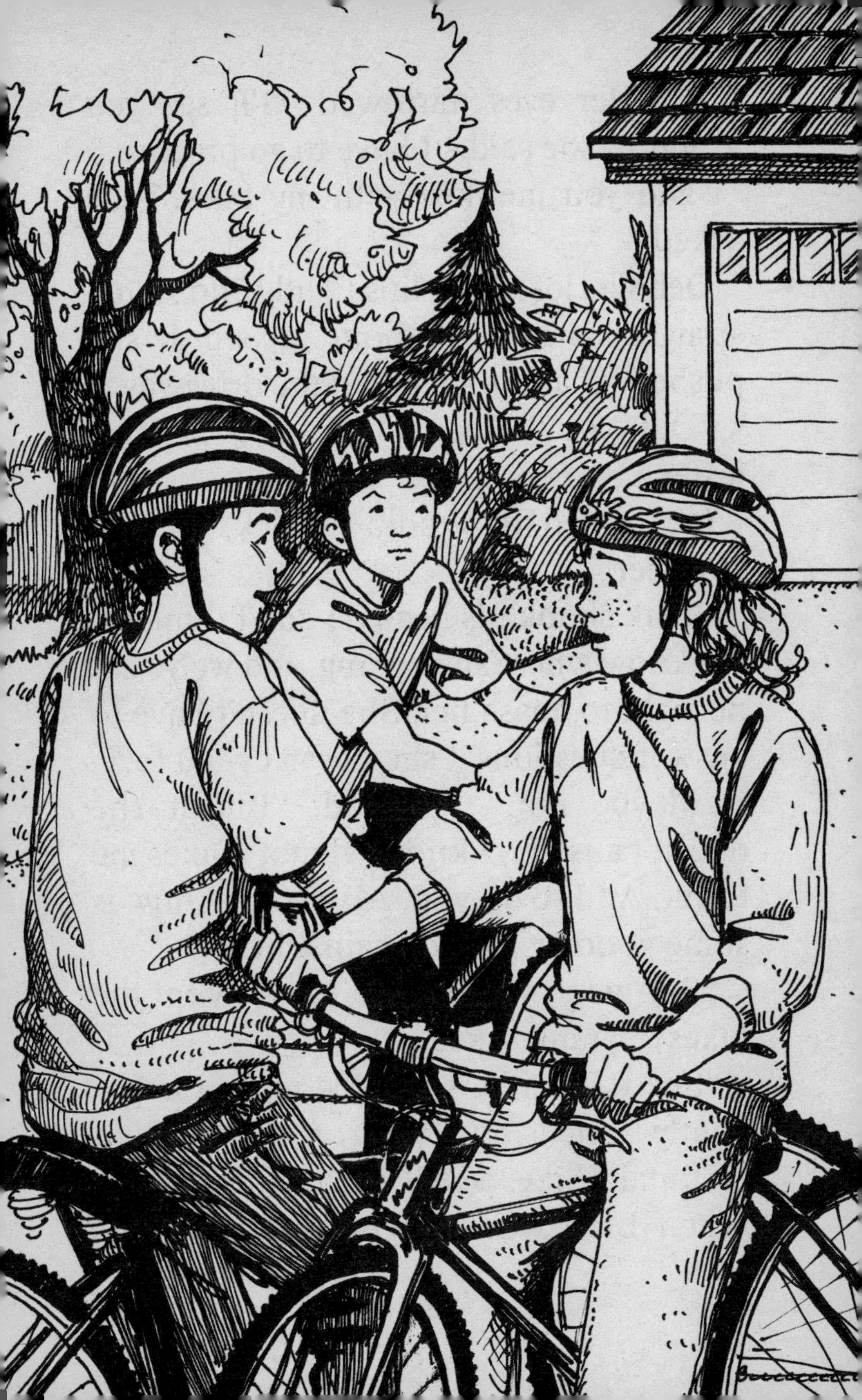

back. Her eyes narrowed. "I'll see you around," she said. "I have to go practice."

"Did you monkey with my bike?" Joe asked.

Debbie closed her lips tightly and stared straight ahead. Without a word she pushed off and rode down the driveway.

"Did you?" Joe called. She pedaled faster.

Joe turned to Frank. "Quick, let's go after her!"

Frank shook his head. "I don't think so. We know where she's going, and we've got no right to chase her. She doesn't have to answer questions if she doesn't want to."

"Maybe not," Joe said. "But if she doesn't answer, I know what it makes me think. And so do you. All we need now is some good evidence against her."

"But why would she mess with the bikes?" Frank asked.

"She told us herself," Joe replied impatiently. "She is totally set on winning that mountain bike. She'll do anything for it. When Brett was bragging yesterday, she believed him. So she set out to wreck his chances."

"Hmm," Frank said. Did that make sense? he wondered. "Then why pick on you?"

Joe's face turned pink. "Er . . . maybe somebody told her *I* had a chance to win. Some other kid, I mean. I wouldn't say it myself. Bragging isn't cool."

Frank laughed. "Right," he said. "Well, you sure won't win if you don't practice."

The Hardys rode back to the park. They got there just as Brett and Zack rode into the woods.

"They must be trying out the new cross-country course," Joe said. "Let's go after them."

A little way into the woods, the path forked. An arrow tacked to a tree pointed left. Just a few yards later another arrow directed them onto a narrow, twisty trail. Frank and Joe rode down into a gully, then up the other side.

The course turned and branched and twisted back on itself. Pretty soon Frank felt maybe not quite lost, but not too sure of where he was, either.

The path forked again. The cardboard arrow pointed right, down a steep, narrow trail.

Joe looked back at Frank. "Hey," he said. "Isn't this the way to the turtle pond?"

Up ahead Frank heard Zack let out a yell. Then Brett yelled, too.

Splash!

5

Zack Takes a Dip

Quick!" Joe shouted to Frank. "Zack and Brett must have fallen into the pond. We have to get them out!"

Joe started to pedal faster. Then he changed his mind. He slowed down and rode more carefully. He didn't want to end up in the water like Zack and Brett.

The narrow dirt track curved around a big bush. Just past the bush it suddenly ended at the muddy edge of the pond. Joe stopped just in time.

"What are you staring at, twerp?" Zack demanded.

Joe did not blame him for sounding cross. Zack and Brett were up to their knees in muddy water. Their jeans and T-shirts were caked with mud. Zack had a streak of green slime on his cheek and neck.

"You guys need a hand?" Frank asked.

Zack scowled. "Not from you, we don't." He picked up his bicycle and started wading toward the bank. The mud he kicked up made the water even murkier.

"Watch out," Joe said. "The pond's full of snapping turtles, you know."

"Baloney," Zack growled. He looked down nervously.

"I'm out of here!" Brett declared. He tried to push past Zack.

"Hey, look out!" Zack yelled. His foot slipped on the muddy bottom. He started to fall. He grabbed Brett's arm.

Plonk! Brett and Zack sat down in the water. Joe and Frank dodged the splash. Joe bit his lip to keep from laughing.

"I'll get you Hardys!" Zack shouted. "You just wait!"

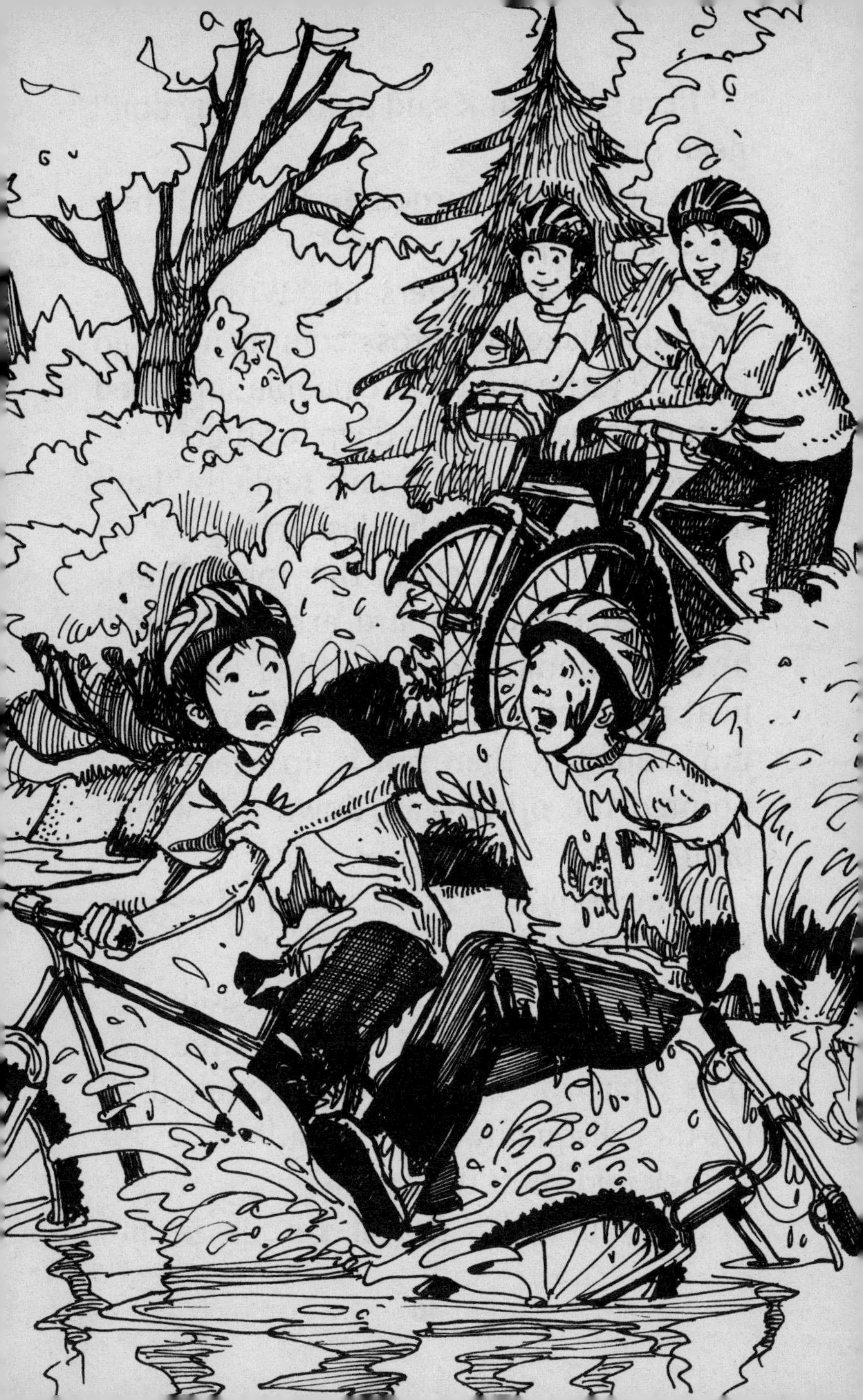

"Let's go," Frank said to Joe. "They don't need our help."

Joe and Frank turned and walked their bikes up the path.

"I don't get it," Joe said. "Why did the officials make the cross-country race go into the turtle pond? Are people supposed to ride across? It's too deep for that."

"Good question," Frank replied. "Let's take a good look at that last arrow."

When they reached the fork, Frank peered at the cardboard arrow. Excited, he said, "Look, there's another tack hole near the bottom edge. What if somebody unfastened it, then put it up again so it pointed the other way, down the wrong path?"

"Somebody?" Zack snarled from behind them. "*You*, you mean!"

"Talk about dirty tricks!" Brett added.

"I'm going to go tell the jamboree officials what you did," Zack threatened. "I bet they disqualify both of you!"

Zack and Brett rode away.

"Do you think they'll get us in hot

water?" Joe asked Frank. "I don't want to be thrown out of the jamboree."

"Don't worry about hot water," Frank assured him. "Zack is full of hot air. All we have to do is find out who really switched the arrow."

"Great," Joe said. "But how? Do you see any clues? What about footprints?"

Frank studied the ground. Then he shook his head. "It's too scuffed under the tree. But look, Joe. There's another tack hole in the trunk, higher up than the arrow. That must be where the arrow was before."

"Why put the arrow lower?" Joe wondered. "I know! Whoever changed it is *shorter* than the grown-up who laid out the course."

"So it's kids we're looking for," Frank said. "I bet they'll try again. I wish we could hide in the bushes overnight and catch them in the act."

Joe chuckled. "I can just hear you trying to sell that idea to Mom and Dad."

Joe and Frank rode back to the playground area. Tony had set up a slalom course again, but no one was practicing. A bunch of kids were standing in a clump talking. They looked upset.

Tanya noticed the Hardys and called, "Hey, did you hear? The Bike Jamboree might be called off!"

Joe and Frank got off their bikes and joined the group. "That's terrible," Frank said. "Why?"

"Zack and Brett," Tony said. "They told the sponsor, Mr. Balfrey, about all these dirty tricks. He's worried somebody will get hurt."

"I think he's worried about bad publicity for his bike shop," Tanya said.

"Whatever," Tony said. "He's worried, and he says he might back out."

"We've got to do something," Joe whispered to Frank. "We can't let them call off the jamboree!"

"Then we'd better find out who's behind the dirty tricks," Frank said. "I've got an idea. Let's see if Mike can help us."

Their friend Mike Mendez was a technical whiz. He loved inventing new gadgets.

Frank and Joe told him about somebody changing the arrow on the cross-country course. "Can you think of a way to catch anyone who tries it again?" Joe asked.

Mike scratched his head. "What about a noose that grabs their ankle and hauls them up into the tree?" he suggested.

"That's too rough," Frank said. "And what if it grabbed somebody else by mistake? Besides, all we really need is to find out who it is. Can we take their picture?"

"Hmmm . . ." Mike said. "You know that robot burglar detector I made for the science fair? It's got a camera that's set off by an electric eye. We can use that. When do you need it?"

"Right now!" Frank and Joe said at the same time.

"Or sooner," Frank added, with a grin.

"Come on home with me," Mike said. "Let's see what we can do."

Mike's workshop was crammed with stuff. He dug through a carton. Frank noticed a hockey mask, an aquarium pump, a video-game controller, and a jar of rubber washers.

"Where do you get all this stuff?" Joe asked.

Mike chuckled. "People throw it away. I recycle it. Okay, here's the robot. I thought it was in this box."

"Wow, thanks, Mike," Frank said. He looked at his watch. "Let's go set it up. We've got just enough time before dinner."

The next morning after breakfast, Joe and Frank picked up Mike. They went to the park and followed the cross country course.

When they reached the fork near the turtle pond, Joe said, "Look! The arrow's been changed again!"

Mike dashed over to the bush where they had hidden the robot. "Three shots gone," he announced. "Great!"

"Let's take the robot over to Bay Street," Frank said. "There's a place that develops film right away."

"Right away" turned out to be half an

hour later. At last the photos were ready. Frank took them out of the yellow envelope. He looked at the first one and gasped.

There, stretching up to switch the arrow, was Chet's kid sister, Iola!

6

Photo Finish

Iola wants to wreck the jamboree?" Chet exclaimed. "I don't believe it!"

Joe and Frank were with Chet in his front yard. They had ridden to his house, looking for Iola. She wasn't home. Chet thought she was out bird-watching.

Joe felt bad. He liked Iola. "We've got proof," he said. He showed Chet the photo of Iola switching the arrow.

Chet studied the picture. He seemed to hope it wasn't really his sister. It was.

"Maybe she's putting the sign back the way it should be?" Chet suggested. "No, I guess not."

Chet pulled on his blue bike helmet. "We'd better find her, fast. Who knows what she's up to now?"

They rode to the park. Some grown-ups were busy setting up the judges' stand for that afternoon. The first event was due to start at two o'clock. A bunch of kids were hanging around, watching. Joe and Frank asked them if they'd seen Iola.

"I did," a third grader said. "In the woods, near the picnic area. She was looking at birds."

The Hardys, along with Chet, hurried to the picnic area. No Iola.

Joe peered at the dirt path. "Look, footprints!" he said. "They go that way."

Frank laughed. "I see footprints, too," he announced. "But they go the other way."

"*Shh-h-h!*" someone hissed.

They all jumped with surprise. Joe looked around. Iola was sitting in the crook of a nearby tree. She was at least six feet up. The tree's leaves hid her.

"Quiet! You'll scare the birds away," she whispered.

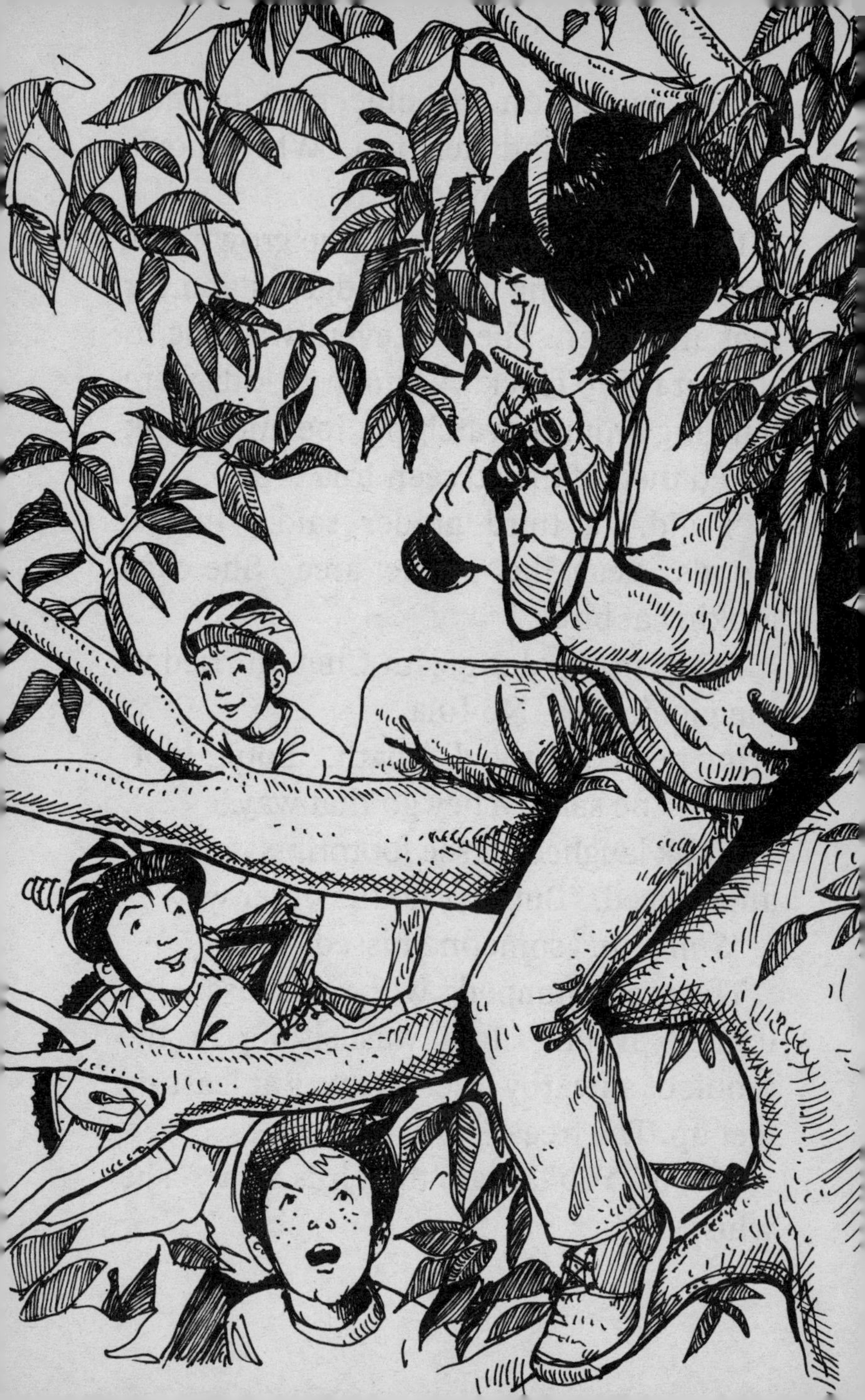

"Get down from there," Chet whispered back. He cleared his throat. In a normal voice, he said, "We have to talk to you."

"Can't you wait?" Iola asked. "This is important. I saw a cardinal. I think it'll come back."

"*This* is important, Iola," Frank said. "It's about the way you tried to mess up the cross-country course."

Iola's eyes grew wide. "Oh," she said softly. "Okay. Here I come."

She scrambled down the tree and came over to them. Joe thought she looked scared.

"Why'd you do it, Sis?" Chet demanded.

"It was the nest," Iola said. "I watched the people marking the course. It went right next to a bush with a nest in it. Frank, you remember the other day? When you crashed into a bush?"

"I sure do," Frank said. He rubbed the scratches on his arm.

"I got worried," Iola said. "What if that happened again, but near the nest? The

49

baby birds might get hurt. So I changed the arrow."

Joe grinned. "And sent Zack and Brett right into the turtle pond," he said. "I hope they didn't poison the turtles!"

"How did you catch me?" Iola wondered.

Frank showed her the pictures and explained.

"I *knew* I heard something," Iola said. "But I was in a big hurry. I couldn't go look. What if it was a bear?"

"What I don't get," Chet said, "is why you put the gum on Brett's brake the other day. That was a dirty trick."

Iola's jaw dropped. "I never!" she wailed. "I wasn't even there!"

"Hey, that's right," Joe said. "She wasn't. And you didn't monkey with my bike seat after school yesterday?"

"I wouldn't do that," Iola replied. "You're my friend."

Joe believed her. He looked at Frank. "What now?" he asked.

"We go tell somebody about that nest,"

Frank replied. "Then we figure out who's trying to ruin the jamboree."

"We'd better hurry," Joe pointed out. "Before Mr. Balfrey decides to cancel it."

Near the judges' stand, they spotted a woman with a clipboard. The badge on her jacket read, Joan Magnusson, Judge. She noticed them looking at her. "Can I help you kids?" she asked.

"It's about the cross-country race," Frank said. "Iola, tell her about the nest."

Iola explained. Joe noticed she didn't mention shifting the arrow.

Ms. Magnusson nodded. "I see," she said. "Yes, that is a problem, isn't it? I'm glad you brought it to our attention."

Iola's face lit up. "Then you'll do something?" she asked. "You'll send the race a different way?"

"Oh, I expect so," Ms. Magnusson said with a smile. "I'll have to tell Mr. Orton about it. Cross-country is his event."

Ms. Magnusson walked over to a man in a blue shirt and spoke to him. He listened, then nodded. Ms. Magnusson looked back at Iola and gave her a thumbs-up.

"Hey, thanks, guys," Iola said to Joe and Frank. "Now I can go back and hunt for that cardinal."

"I'm glad it's not her," Chet said after Iola had left. "But I wish we still had a suspect."

"We do," Joe pointed out. "Debbie. She acted very funny yesterday when we tried to question her about my bike saddle."

"She has a good reason, too," Frank added. "And she lives near Brett. She could have sneaked over and flattened his tires. Hmmm . . . There's something I need to check."

Chet and Joe followed Frank to a pay phone. He got Brett's number and dialed it.

"Mrs. Marks?" he said. "This is Frank Hardy. Is Brett there? Oh. No, I just wanted to warn him. He shouldn't leave his bike outside at night. Somebody's been going around messing with people's bikes."

Frank listened for a few moments. Then he hung up. He gave Joe and Chet a puzzled look.

"Brett's mom says he always puts his bike in the garage," he said. "And they lock their garage at night."

"Then how did Debbie get in to let the air out of Brett's tires?" Chet asked.

"Good question," Frank replied.

"There she is, over by the basketball court," Joe said, pointing. "You think we can get her to answer our questions this time?"

"We can try," Frank said.

Two officials were laying out the obstacle course. It was much harder and more twisty than the slalom everybody had been practicing. Kids started lining up to try out the course. Debbie was first in line.

Frank, Joe, and Chet went up to her.

"We want to talk to you," Frank said.

Debbie scowled. "Not now," she snapped. "Can't you see I'm busy?"

"Okay, kids," one of the officials called. "The course is open for practice."

Debbie climbed on her bike and pushed off. She rode so slowly and carefully that Joe was sure her bike would fall over. At each turn, she picked up speed until she was around, then slowed down to head into the next turn.

"Hey, she is good!" one of the kids waiting said.

"Wait a minute," an older boy said. "That bike—it's not hers. It belongs to a friend of mine. He's out of town."

The boy cupped his hands around his mouth. "Come back here!" he shouted to Debbie. "You stole that bike! Stop, thief!"

7

On the Run

"Stop, thief!"

Debbie heard the shout and looked back. Frank was only a couple of dozen feet away from her. He saw her face turn pale. For a moment her bike wobbled. Then she stood up on the pedals and pushed with all her weight. The bike shot forward.

"Grab her!" Zack yelled. "She's getting away!"

Debbie steered past two kids and headed toward the park entrance.

The crowd let out a howl and ran after

Debbie. Zack was at the head of the pack.

"Come on," Frank urged Joe. "We don't want anybody to get hurt."

Frank and Joe sprinted across the field. They had not gone far when Brett raced past them on his bike. He almost hit them.

"Out of my way, nerds!" he yelled. Soon he overtook the mob of runners.

"Are they all nuts?" Joe panted. "What did she do?"

Frank didn't answer. He was starting to get a pain in his side. He pressed his hand to the place and put on more speed. He and Joe were catching up to the other runners.

Up ahead Debbie still had a good lead on Brett. She turned onto a walkway that led out of the park.

"Uh-oh," Frank gasped.

A woman with two little kids in a stroller came into the park. The double stroller took up the whole width of the sidewalk. Debbie could not get past. She was about to crash into the stroller!

Just in time Debbie swerved off the walk

and braked to a stop. Moments later Brett caught up to her. He grabbed her handlebars.

"You're not going anywhere," Brett growled. "Dirty thief!"

"I'm not—" Debbie started to say.

The clump of runners arrived. They made a circle around the two bike riders.

"Brett, you let her alone!" Tanya yelled.

"What's going on here?" an adult voice demanded.

Frank glanced back over his shoulder. Ms. Magnusson, the jamboree official, hurried over to the group of kids.

"That girl stole somebody's bike," one kid said.

"She tried to run away," another said. "But we stopped her."

"Who is the owner of this bicycle?" Ms. Magnusson asked. She looked around the circle.

No one answered. Then the older boy said, "It belongs to a guy I know. I recognized it."

Frank pushed forward. "Debbie?" he

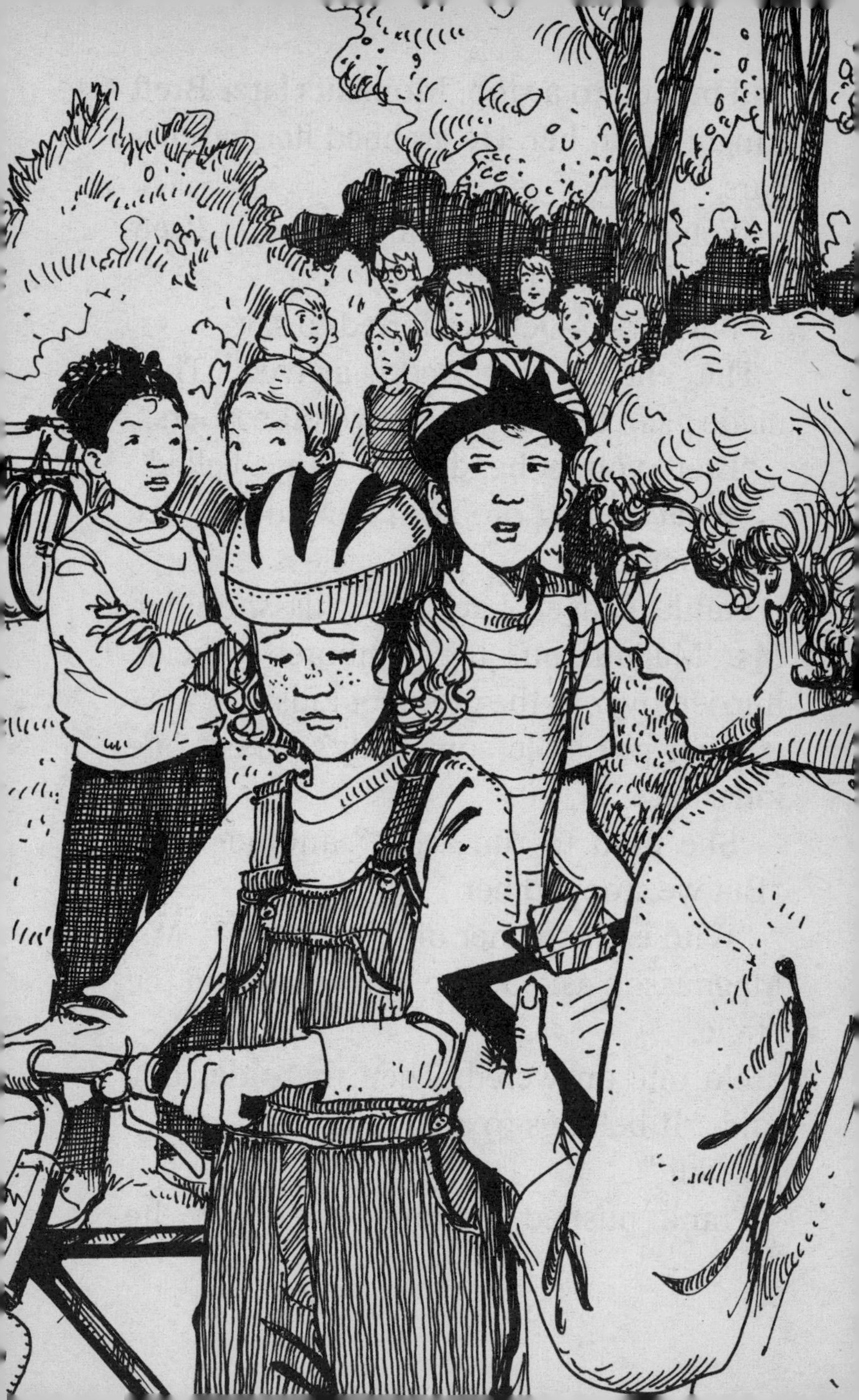

said. "What's the story? Is this your bike?"

Debbie stared at the ground. In a soft voice she said, "No. It's my neighbor Brendan's bike. He said I could borrow it while he's away."

"Then why did you run away?" Frank asked.

"I got scared," Debbie told him. "It's not my bike, and Brendan's not around to say it's okay. What would people think?"

"Where's your bike?" Joe asked.

Debbie's cheeks turned pink. "It got stolen, just before we moved here."

"That's a shame," Tanya said.

"My mom and dad want to get me a new one," Debbie continued. "But moving all the way across the country costs a fortune."

"How do we know she's not making this up?" Zack demanded.

Frank turned to the older boy. "The guy you say owns the bike. What's his name?" he asked.

"Er . . ." The boy looked away. "Brendan. I don't know his last name."

"She still could have stolen it," Brett insisted.

Debbie put her hand on Ms. Magnusson's arm. "My mom has the number where Brendan's staying," she said. "It's at home. You can call him and ask. He'll tell you it's okay."

Ms. Magnusson patted Debbie's hand. "I don't think I'll need to do that, dear," she said.

She turned to the boy who had accused Debbie. "You should be more careful," she said. "It's a serious matter to call somebody a thief."

"Well, it *wasn't* her bike," the boy muttered. "How was I supposed to know she borrowed it?"

"Some apology," Joe said to Frank.

The crowd started to drift back to the obstacle course. Frank, Joe, and Chet stayed behind. So did Tanya.

"Debbie?" Frank said. "Can we ask you a couple of questions?"

Debbie's face hardened. "You still think I did something wrong, don't you?"

"No," Joe replied. "But we can't help wondering. A kid saw you with a bike tool after school yesterday. That was right after somebody loosened my saddle."

"Brendan's bike is a little too big for me," Debbie told him. "I mean, look at it. I wanted to leave it the way Brendan had it. But I couldn't. I had to lower the seat. I was lucky. There was a special wrench in the tool pouch."

Frank studied Brendan's bike. "Joe, look," he said. "This is an Italian bike. The nuts are metric sizes. But yours is an American make. Everything's in fractions of an inch."

"Hey, that's right," Joe said. "Debbie couldn't have loosened my saddle post. Her bike tool wouldn't have fit the nut."

"Yay!" Tanya cheered.

"I'm convinced," Chet said.

Debbie beamed.

Joe said, "There's just one other thing."

Debbie's face fell.

"The bubble gum," Joe continued. "Remember? You said you had a piece in your pack. But when you looked, it wasn't there. You told us you'd left it at home. Was that the truth?"

"Well . . ." Debbie began. She blinked a couple of times. "No, it wasn't. I know it was there before. Somebody must have sneaked it out of my pack."

"And stuck it on Brett's brake," Frank said. "Why didn't you tell us?"

Debbie hesitated. Finally she said, "I was afraid it was Tanya. She knew the gum was there. I'd told her."

"Did you?" Tanya said. "I don't remember. But I'd never try to mess up somebody's bike. What if they got hurt?"

"*I* know you wouldn't do that," Debbie said. "But what if other kids thought you did? So I kept my mouth shut."

"Did anyone else hear you tell Tanya about the gum?" Frank asked.

"I don't remember," Debbie said. "Wait—I know Brett and Zack were there. Zack was bragging about his fancy new helmet."

"He would be," Joe muttered.

"Is that all?" Debbie continued. "I really do need to practice for the obstacle course. I bet the line is miles long."

They walked back to the basketball court. Frank asked Debbie, "Did you go by Brett's house the other night?"

Debbie looked surprised. "Brett? I don't even know where he lives. Why?"

"Just wondering," Frank said. He was starting to see a solution to all the mysteries.

There was a long line to practice the obstacle course. Zack was number two. He was dangling his new, bright blue helmet by the strap. He saw Frank and Joe join the line.

"Hey, look, everybody," he sneered. "It's the Clueless Brothers!"

Joe turned to Frank. "I hear Zack got bit by a snake," he said loudly.

Frank played along. "Really?"

"Uh-huh," Joe said. "The snake died."

The other kids in line laughed. Zack gave Frank and Joe a very dirty look.

The girl in front of Zack rode off. It was

almost his turn. He clapped his helmet on his head and started to get on his bike.

"Yeow!" Zack suddenly yelled.

Frank looked at Zack and gasped. Zack had icky red goo running down his forehead and cheeks. The goo looked just like blood!

8

The Telltale Squeeze

Joe and Frank ran toward Zack. Was he badly hurt?

Zack tore off his helmet and threw it on the ground. Like his face, his hair was covered with red goo.

Zack reached up and scrubbed at his head. He stared at the thick red stuff, then wiped his hand on the grass.

"Okay, what clown did this?" Zack asked loudly. "Wait till I get my hands on him!"

A tall man in khakis and a blue jacket rushed over. Joe recognized him. He was

Don Balfrey. He owned Balfrey's Bike Shop. He was the main sponsor of the Bike Jamboree.

Mr. Balfrey pulled an orange cloth from his hip pocket and wiped Zack's face. He looked at the cloth, then sniffed it.

"Ketchup!" he blurted. "I was sure you were bleeding. That's it, I'm pulling out! The Bike Jamboree is canceled!"

Canceled? The crowd of kids groaned.

"Wait," Joe said. "Mr. Balfrey? If we find out who played this trick on Zack, will you let the jamboree go on?"

"Please?" Frank added.

"You're Fenton Hardy's kids, aren't you?" Mr. Balfrey replied. "I've heard of your dad. Well, if I can be sure the event won't be ruined by more dirty tricks . . ."

"Thanks, Mr. Balfrey," Joe said. He turned around. "Hey, everybody! Look around. See if you can spot any empty ketchup packs on the ground."

"Why don't you tell them where to look?" Zack asked in a nasty voice. "Your detective act doesn't fool me. It was you guys who put the ketchup in my helmet."

"Don't be such a dope," Frank said. "When did you wear it last?"

"Um—before we chased Debbie," Zack said. "And no, it wasn't full of ketchup!"

"We came back after you and the others," Joe pointed out. "We couldn't have done it. But someone did."

"Hey, Joe, Frank," Chet called. "Look at this!"

Chet pointed at a blue backpack. It had a big red smear on it near the zipper. Joe and Frank bent down to get a closer look.

"Get away from there," Brett yelled. "That's mine!"

"How about opening it?" Frank asked.

"Jump in the lake," Brett retorted.

"Go ahead, Brett. Open it," Zack said.

Brett gave Frank and Joe a sullen look. He unzipped the pack and held it open.

Joe peered inside. He saw a dirty T-shirt, a pair of socks, a bike wrench—and a squeeze bottle of ketchup. Joe grabbed it and held it up.

"That's not mine," Brett insisted. "You

planted it. You're trying to frame me! Why would I pull a trick on my buddy?"

"I know why," Chet declared. He held up his bike helmet. "My helmet and Zack's were both lying on the ground. And they're pretty much the same color. You were trying to play a trick on me, but you made a mistake."

"You made a few mistakes," Frank said. "Like claiming somebody let the air out of your bike tires the other night."

"What about it?" Brett snapped. "They did."

Frank shook his head. "Uh-uh. Your mom says you always put your bike in the garage. And the garage is locked at night."

Brett raised his clenched fists. "You leave my mom out of this!" he shouted.

"Okay," Joe responded. "What about the bubble gum on your brake? It wasn't there when you left your bike. And you ran back before anybody else. You're the only one who could have stuck it there."

"But why would he mess up his own bike?" Tanya wondered.

"So nobody would suspect him when he messed with other people's bikes," Frank explained.

Brett stuck out his chin. "You can't prove a thing!" he declared.

Joe looked at Brett. The right leg of his jeans looked darker in one spot.

"Oh, yeah?" Joe said. He turned to Mr. Balfrey. "Can I borrow your cloth? And some water?"

"Here," Debbie said. She handed Joe her water bottle.

Joe took the orange cloth and dampened a clean corner. Then he rubbed it on the spot on Brett's jeans. It came away red.

"After you squirted ketchup in Zack's helmet, you wiped your hand off on your pants leg," Joe said.

"Is this true?" Mr. Balfrey demanded.

Brett stared at the cloth. His chin stuck out more than ever.

"None of your business," Brett shouted. "And you can keep your stupid Bike Jamboree. Who needs it?"

Brett grabbed his bike and got on. Then he

turned and pointed his finger at Joe and Frank. "You watch out, you two," he snarled. "I'm going to fix you both, and good!"

Brett rode away. There was a short silence.

"If you ask me," Chet said, "the Clues Brothers just fixed *him*."

Debbie grinned. "And good!" she added.

"Okay, boys. Let's get a shot of you," Mr. Hardy said. He aimed the camera at them.

"Wait," Frank said. "We need Chet in the picture, too."

Joe had just finished the cross-country race. He was muddy all over. He had torn his shirtsleeve on a tree branch, but he didn't care. He had come in second, just behind a boy who was in seventh grade. That meant he got the ribbon for the elementary school age group.

Frank was pleased, too. His point total in the obstacle course was one of the highest so far. But there were still a few more contestants—and one was Debbie.

"I can't believe Chet won first place," Joe said. "He never even let on he was going to enter."

Chet came up, wheeling his bike. "Let's hear it for the champ," he said. "Taa-daa!"

Joe and Frank burst out laughing. The prize Chet had won was for the funniest bike. They could see why. He had spent lunch time decorating it. He had used crepe paper to make the wheels look like giant pepperoni pizzas. A big cardboard ice cream cone was taped to the handlebars.

Mr. Hardy snapped their picture. Then the three friends went over to watch the end of the obstacle course. Debbie was already on the course. She glided around one tough curve after another.

"She makes it look easy," Chet remarked.

"Believe me," Frank replied. "It's not." He could see his chance of winning the event vanishing. He was sorry for it, but he was also happy to watch Debbie's ride. When she finished, he was the first one to clap.

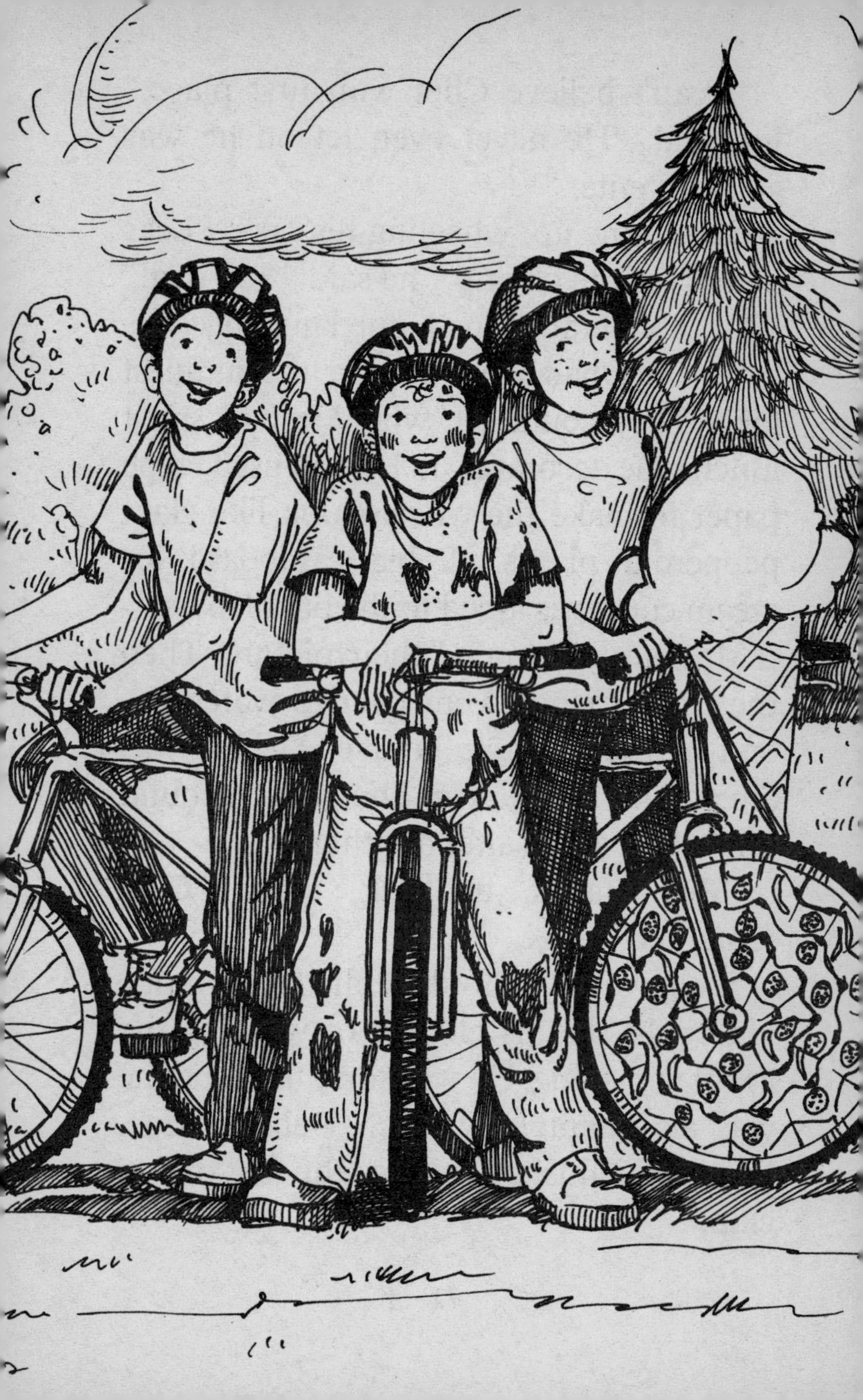

A few minutes later, everyone got a chance to clap. Mr. Balfrey gave out ribbons to each of the winners. Then he announced that all the contestants would be awarded a special Bayport Bike Jamboree T-shirt.

"And now," he said, "the moment we've been waiting for. The grand prize winner, based on a first-rate run in the cross country and an almost perfect score in the obstacle course, is . . . Debbie Marzenik! Come on up, Debbie."

The whole crowd cheered. Mr. Balfrey wheeled forward a brand-new mountain bike and gave it to Debbie. She gulped and wiped her eyes. Then she moved closer to the microphone.

"Thank you, thank you," she said. "And a really special thank you to the guys who made it possible. Let's have three cheers for two amazing detectives. Frank and Joe Hardy—the Clues Brothers!"

EASY TO READ—FUN TO SOLVE!

**Meet up with suspense and mystery
in The Hardy Boys® are:**

THE CLUES™
BROTHERS

Available from Minstrel® Books
Published by Pocket Books

2389

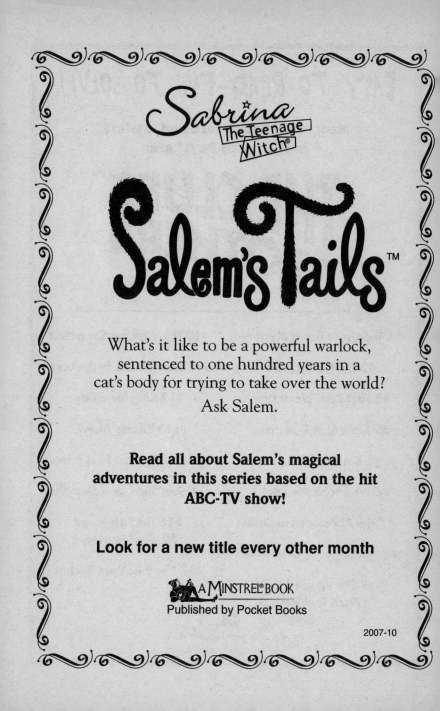

Sabrina The Teenage Witch®

Salem's Tails™

What's it like to be a powerful warlock,
sentenced to one hundred years in a
cat's body for trying to take over the world?
Ask Salem.

**Read all about Salem's magical
adventures in this series based on the hit
ABC-TV show!**

Look for a new title every other month

A MINSTREL® BOOK
Published by Pocket Books

2007-10